CALUMET CITY PUBLIC LIBRARY
3 1613 00471 4526

W9-CFB-926

First published in the United States in 2013 by Chronicle Books LLC · First published in Switzerland in 2012 under the title *Ligne 135*, by Editions La Joie de lire SA, 5 chemin Neuf, 1207 Genève-Switzerland

Library of Congress Cataloging-in-Publication Data available · ISBN: 978-1-4521-1934-2 · Manufactured in China · 10 9 8 7 6 5 4 3 2 · Chronicle Books LLC, 680 Second Street, San Francisco, California 94107 · www.chroniclekids.com

LINE 135

By Germano Zullo Illustrated by Albertine

chronicle books · san francisco

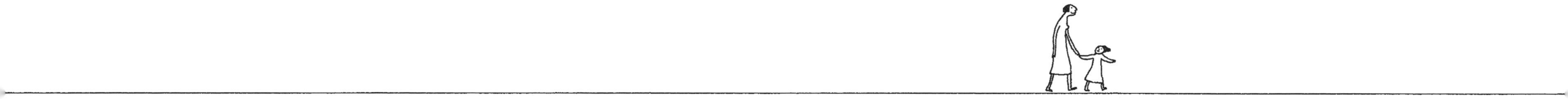

There are two places I belong in the world. The first place I belong is my house in the city.

The second place I belong is my grandmother's house in the country.

HOTEL
SNOB
ZIP
GRAND
MAGASIN

My grandmother lives very far away, practically on the other side of the world.

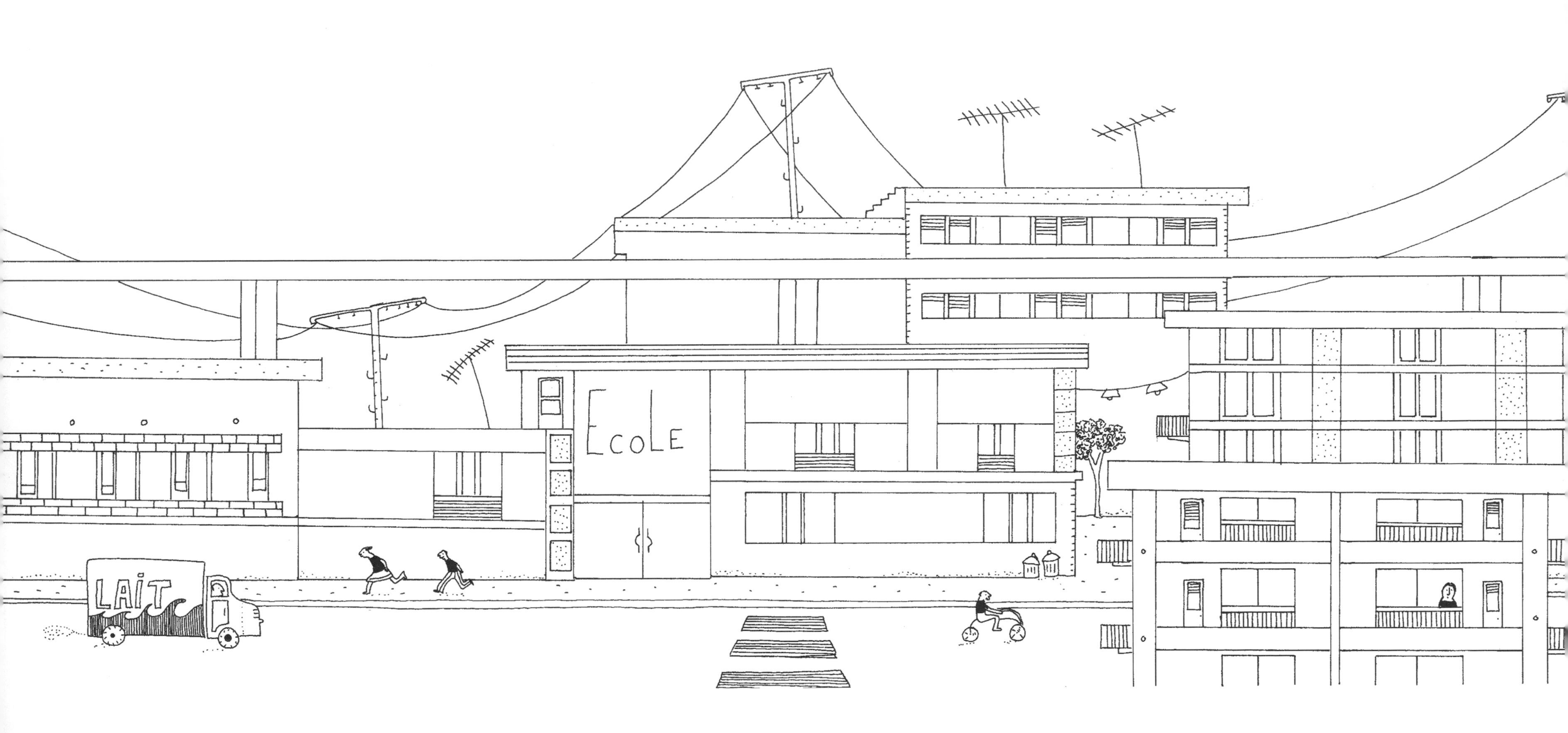
EcoLE
LAiT

When you move between two places, it's called traveling.

One day, I will travel everywhere. I will go here. I will go there. I will go this way and I will go that way. I will know the entire world.

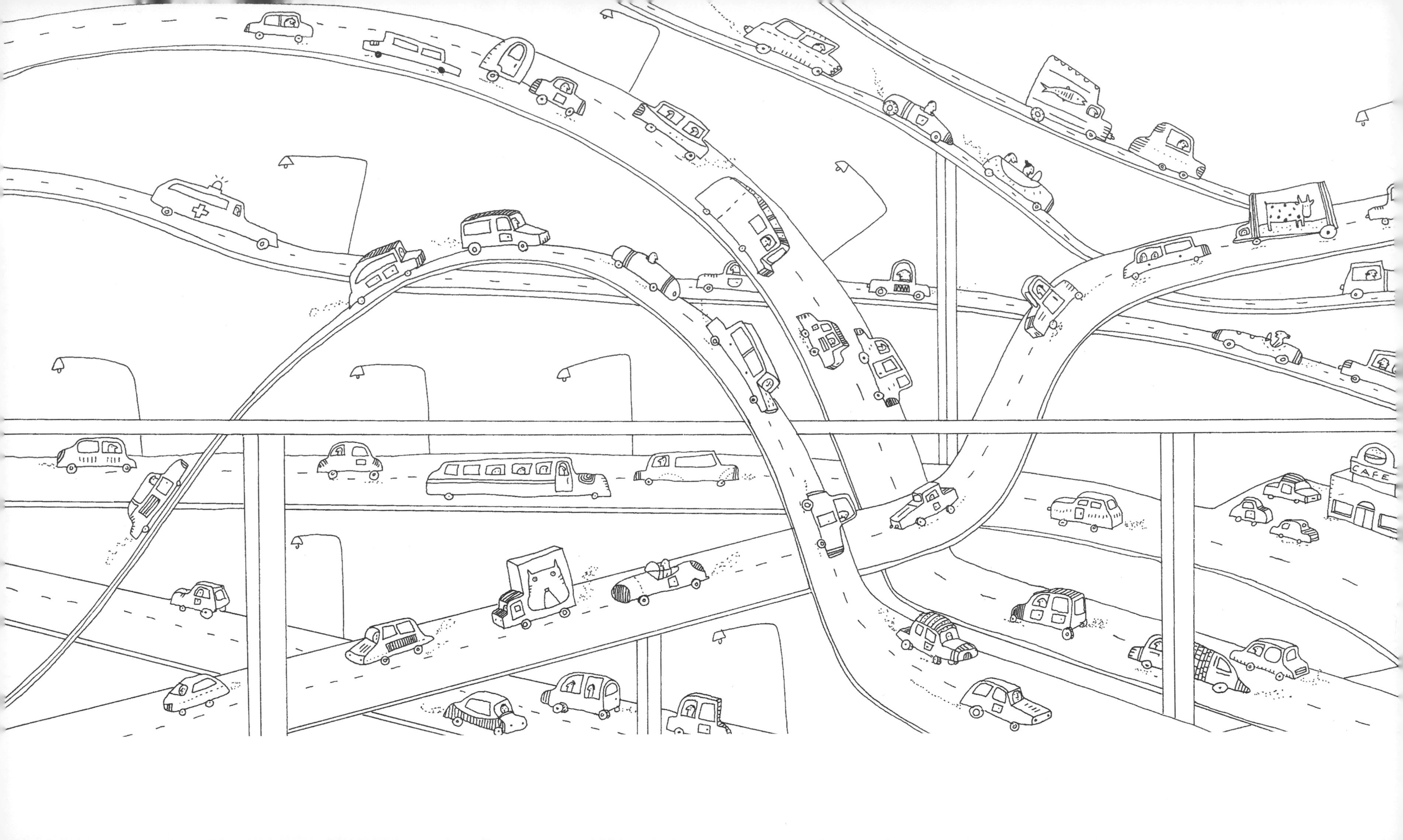
CAFE

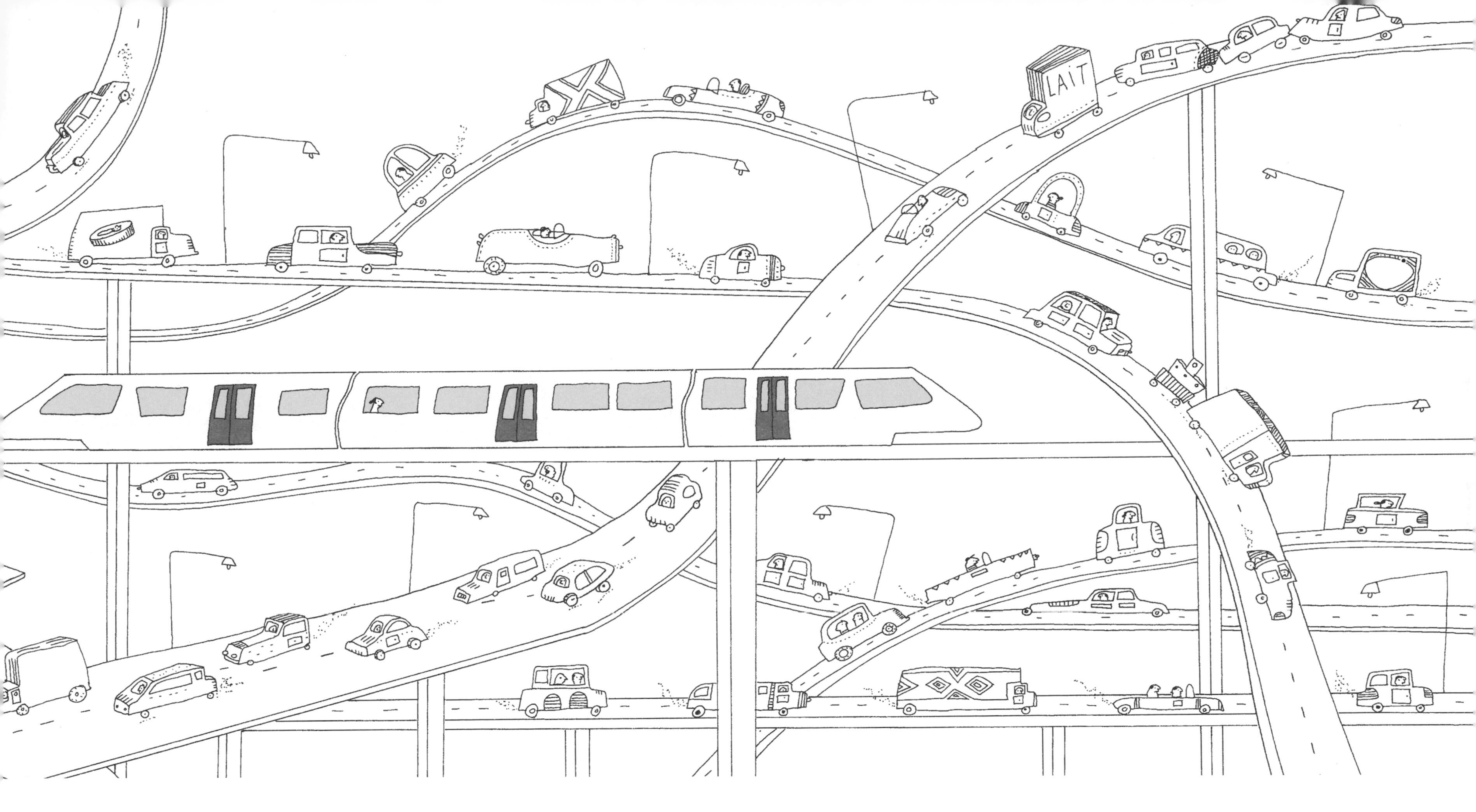

My mother and my grandmother say that this is impossible.

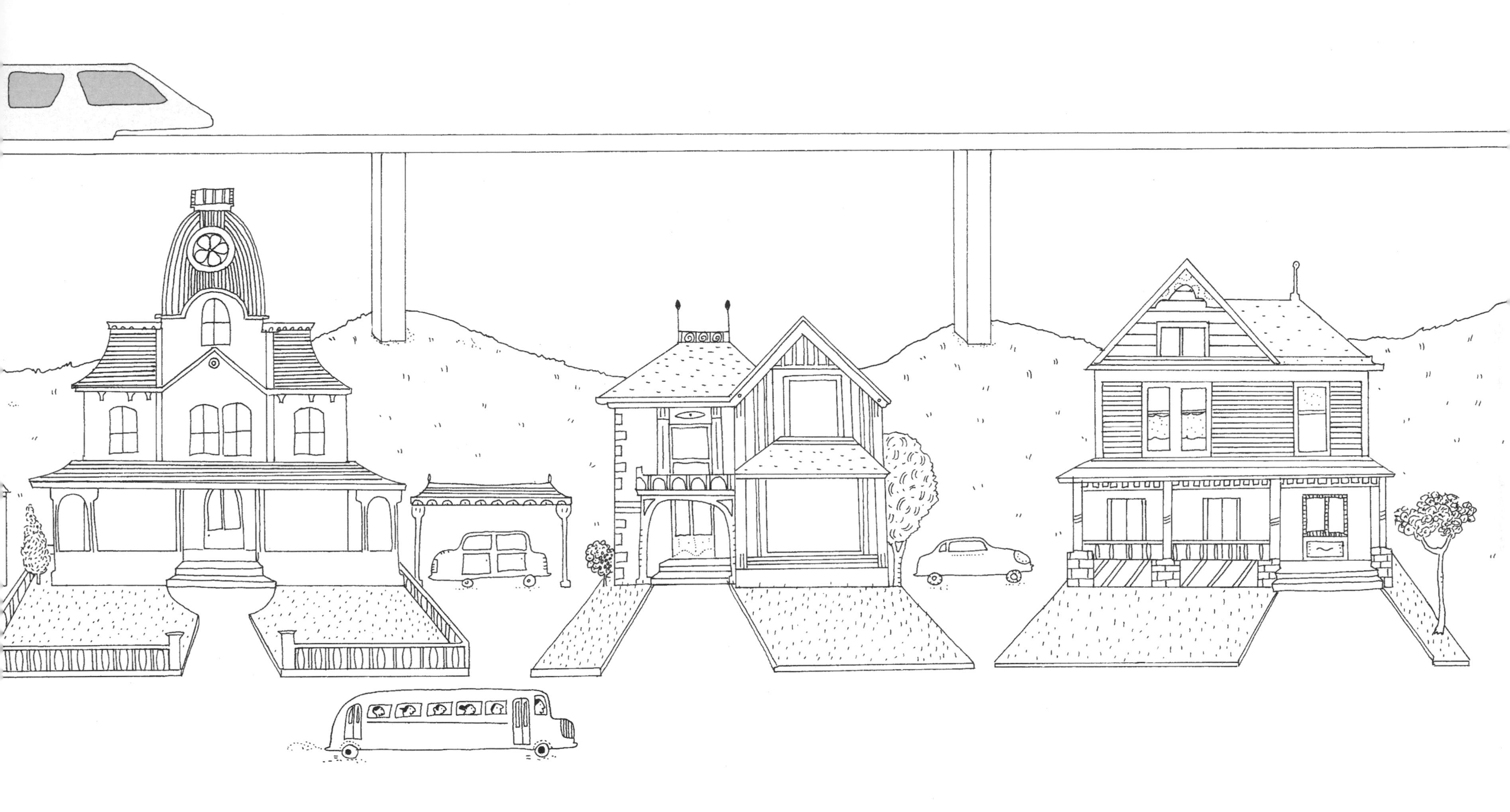

My mother and my grandmother say that I am too small to know the entire world.

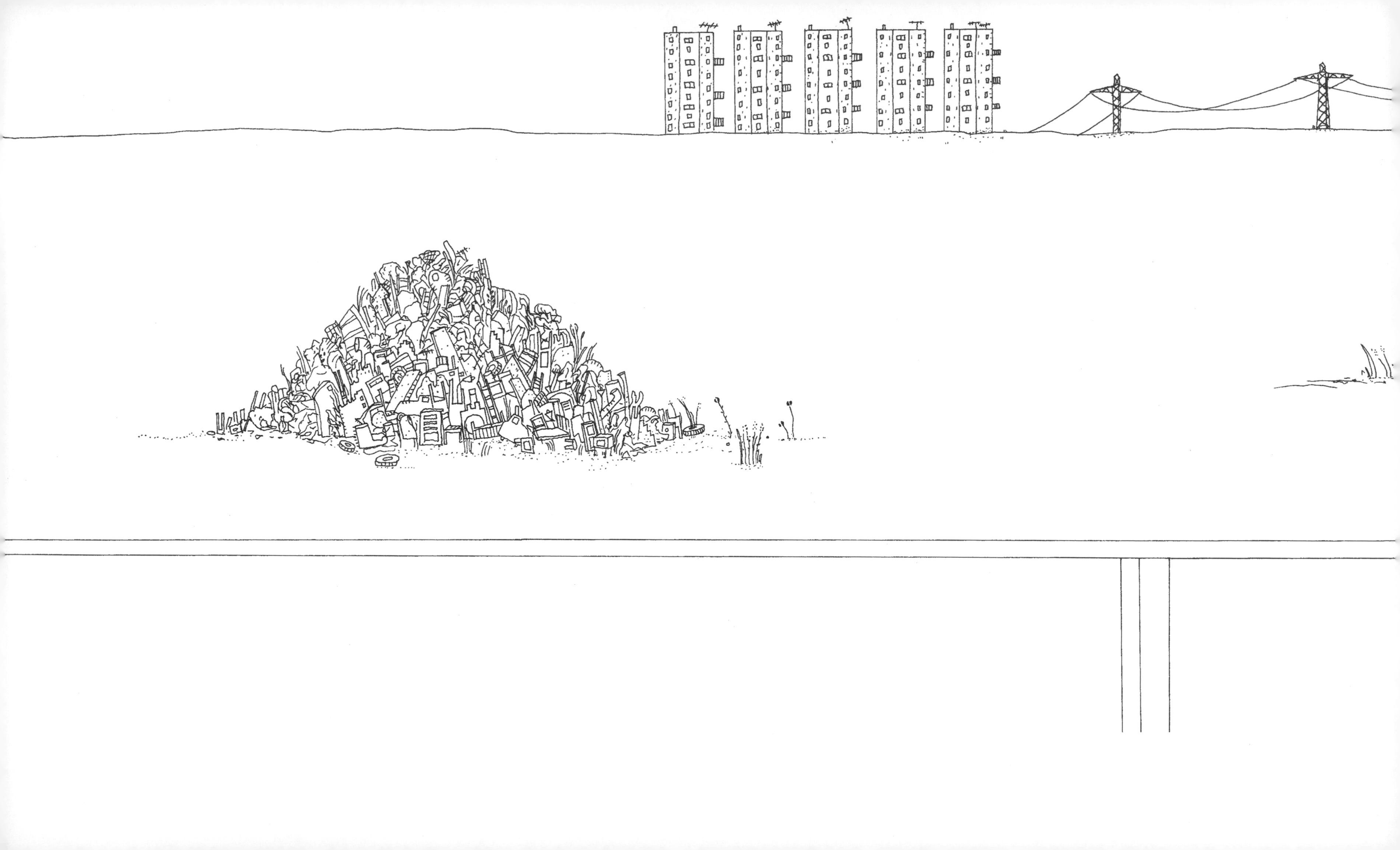

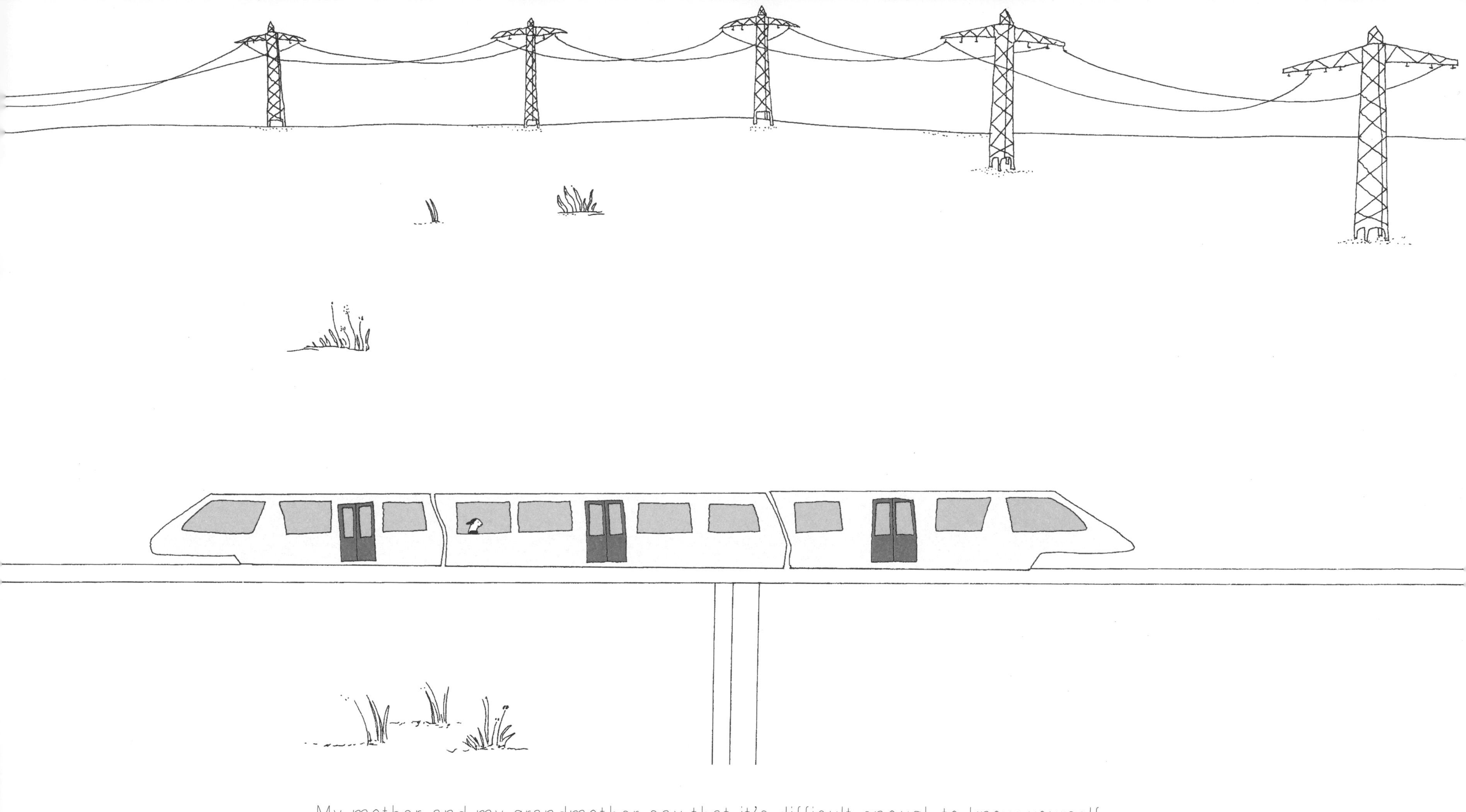

My mother and my grandmother say that it's difficult enough to know yourself.

I don't always understand my mother and my grandmother.

My mother says that when I am big, I will understand things better.

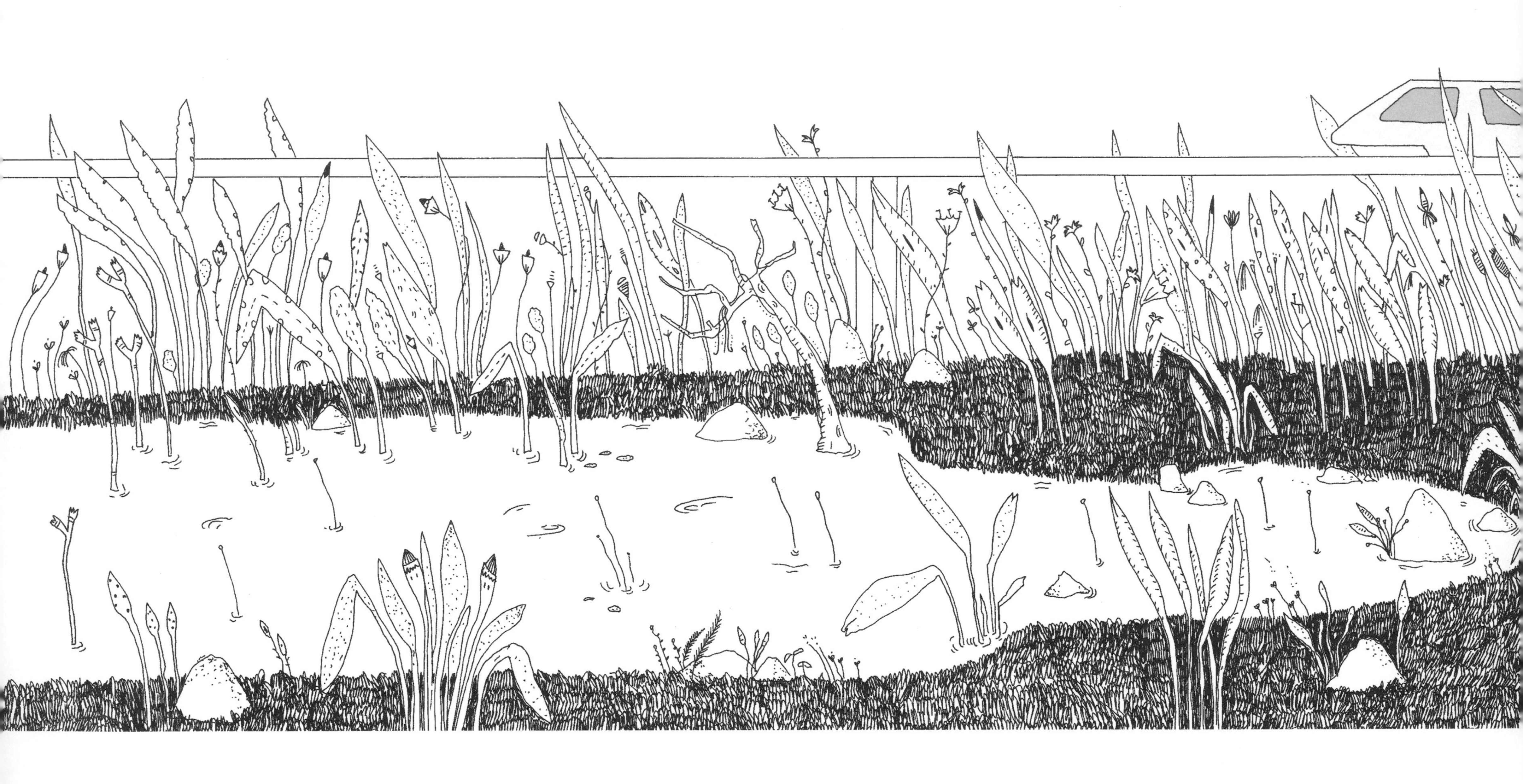

My grandmother says that when I am big, life will pass by very quickly.

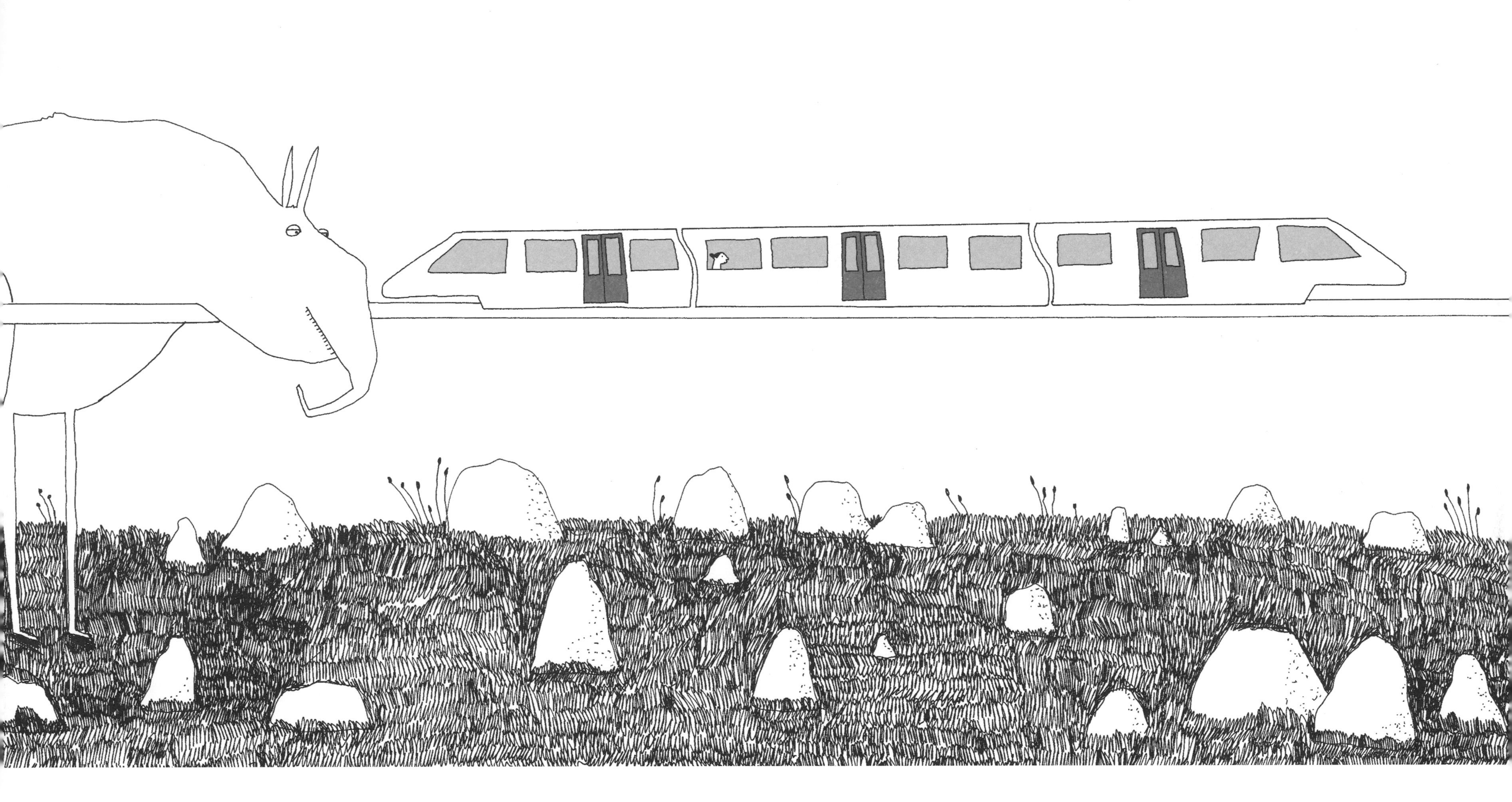

My mother and my grandmother always say, “You’ll see!”

I want to be big so I can understand things better.

But when I am big, I will make sure life moves with me.

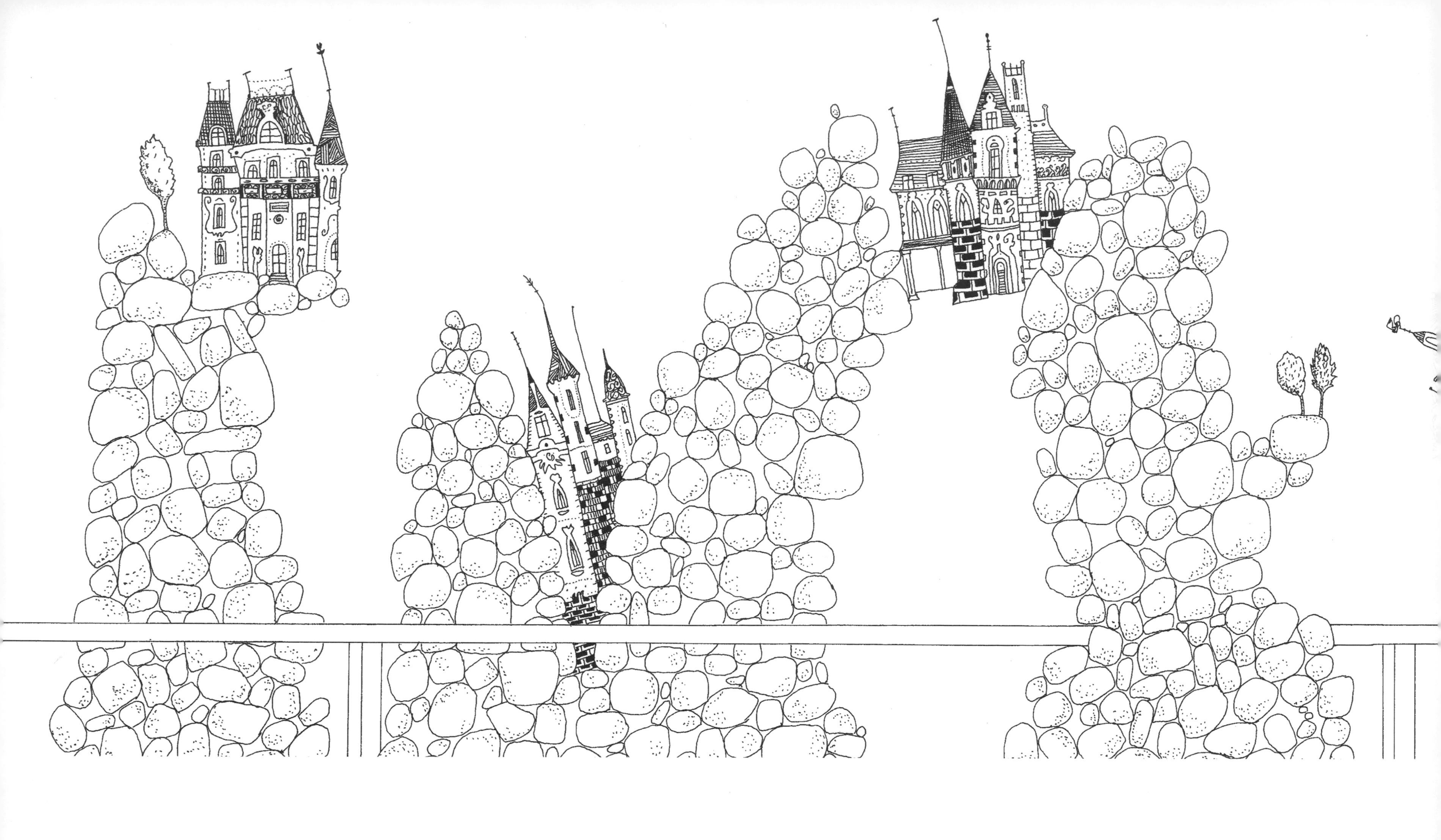

And I *will* go everywhere. I will go here. I will go there. I will go this way and I will go that way. I will know the entire world.

And I will say to my mother and my grandmother: “You see!”

Because my mother and my grandmother have forgotten what I have always known: It *is* possible.